A SIENA BOOK

Siena is an imprint of Parragon Books

Published by Parragon Book Service Ltd.
Units 13-17, Avonbridge Trading Estate,
Atlantic Road, Avonmouth, Bristol BS11 9QD

Produced by The Templar Company plc, Pippbrook Mill,
London Road, Dorking, Surrey RH4 1JE

Designed by Mark Kingsley-Monks

Printed and bound in Italy

ISBN 0-75251-256-0

Pinocchio

Illustrated by Stephen Holmes
Retold by Caroline Repchuk

SIENA

Once upon a time there lived an old carpenter called Geppetto. One day he made a wooden puppet.

"I shall call you Pinocchio," decided Geppetto, "and you shall go to school just like a proper boy." The puppet nodded his head happily. That would be fun!

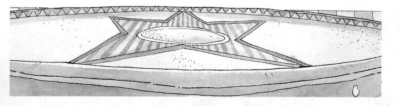

"I should love to be like a real boy," said Pinocchio and he set off down the road — but what was that wonderful music? He followed the sound of trumpets and found himself outside a large tent. It was a puppet theatre, and all at once Pinocchio quite forgot about school.

"Hello!" called the puppets and soon Pinocchio had made two new friends. Suddenly a dark shadow fell over them. It was the puppet master.

"Please don't be angry," begged little Pinocchio. "I was just on my way to school."

"Then you are a good boy," replied the puppet master and he gave the excited puppet five gold coins. Further down the road Pinocchio met two strange creatures, but when they saw his coins their eyes glittered greedily.

"We want those!" they said and they hung him upside down.

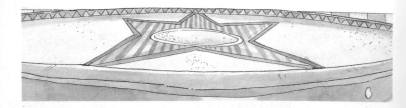

But they did not find his
money for the clever puppet had
hidden it under his tongue. Soon
he was rescued by the Blue Fairy.

"Where is the gold?" she said.

"I lost it," fibbed Pinocchio.
Suddenly his nose began to grow,
and soon it was as long as his
arm! The Fairy laughed.

"You mustn't fib!" she said.

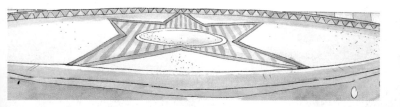

"I will be a good boy and go to school," said Pinocchio, but as he ran down the road what should come along but a large coach full of laughing children. "Come with us!" they cried.

But the coach took them to the Land of Boobies and they were all turned into donkeys! Poor Pinocchio grew long ears and a tail. He was very unhappy and so he decided to run away.

He arrived at the seaside and jumped into the deep blue water. As he bobbed in the waves he just had time to see he was a proper puppet once again before a huge whale swallowed him down in one gulp.

"This is the end for me," sobbed poor Pinocchio as he stumbled around the whale's stomach. But who was that? It was his dear father, Geppetto!

"I came looking for you," cried the old carpenter, "but the whale made a meal of me. Let us escape together."

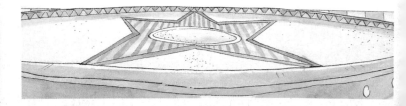

And so they jumped from the whale's mouth and before long were safe and sound at home. Pinocchio worked hard for his father, but he dearly wished that he was a real boy instead of a puppet. Then one night the Blue Fairy made his wish come true.

"Look, father," cried Pinocchio. "I was once a naughty puppet but now I am a real boy!"

Titles in this series include: